W9-CTN-940

One Christmas Story

by stephan j. harper

illustrated by joy steuerwald

INSPIRE PRESS

Published by Inspire Press, Inc.
P.O. Box 33241 Los Gatos, CA 95030

Publisher's Cataloging-in-Publication
(Provided by Quality Books, Inc.)

Harper, Stephan J.
One Christmas story / by Stephan J. Harper ;
illustrated by Joy Steuerwald. -- 1st ed.
p. cm.
SUMMARY: Late Christmas Eve Santa receives help from
an angel named Gloria to bring a special gift to the one
good little girl Santa had forgotten.
Audience: Ages 5-9.
ISBN 0-9741800-0-9

1. North Pole--Juvenile fiction. 2. Santa Claus--
Juvenile fiction. 3. Christmas--Juvenile fiction.
4. Angels--Juvenile fiction. [1. North Pole--Fiction.
2. Santa Claus--Fiction. 3. Christmas-- Fiction.
4. Angels --Fiction.]   I. Steuerwald, Joy. II. Title.

PZ7.H23197On 2003   [E]
                           QB133-1523

Printed in the United States of America

Inspire Press
Los Gatos, CA

online at www.inspirepress.com

For Peggy – S.J.H.

To Mom and Dad, for all their love and support – J.S.

ACKNOWLEDGEMENTS:

Thanks to Antoinette, Susan, Julia - and, of course, Peggy.
Your words of encouragement, advice and constructive
criticism made this a better book. For that, and your kindness,
I am deeply grateful. - S.J.H.

Barry, for being with me through this whole experience.
Tony, for passing this opportunity on to me. Gussy, for
all the computer tips. The Harpers, for their vision. - J.S.

The Publisher wishes to thank Dan Poynter. You had the
master plan; we simply followed your advice and got in
the game. You will always be an inspiration.

And lastly - since we're counting our lucky stars - much
appreciation to Russell Brown of Adobe for leading us to
Dr. Sanjay Sakhuja at Digital Prepress International in
San Francisco who put Marianna Whang on our project.
Marianna, your eye for detail - and your wizardry at the
keyboard - made all the difference.

ate one Christmas Eve when Santa's work was nearly done, and the good little girls and boys on Earth had been rewarded (and the bad little girls and boys given lumps of coal), there remained in the world one good little girl whom Santa had forgotten.

"How could this happen?" Santa was dumbfounded. "And out of presents, too?"

"What will we do? What will we do?" cried Egil. Elves were excitable by nature and always curious.

But for the first time in his long, long life Santa had questions he did not know the answers to. Sure, he had to play along during the season. Little kids would sit on his lap and tell him what they just couldn't live without. As if he hadn't already marked down their names in the big green book and next to each, *clearly written*, exactly what was wanted and where.

"As if!" he huffed.

He was worried though. It was getting late and Mrs. Claus was definite about no overtime this year. He remembered half her baked goodies had gone into the freezer last Christmas, including his favorite blueberry pie that he and Egil hadn't found the time to eat. The pie had to wait under a light frost, with six little lemon cakes, until New Year's Eve when Mrs. Claus popped them back in the oven, sat Santa and Egil down at the kitchen table and made them promise not to work so hard the next year.

"You boys have to work smarter not harder,"
she had said. And that was that—pie, cakes and all.

And now there was this year, night-of-nights again, with everything going like clockwork. The elves had handled the three rushes so well that Santa sent e-mail at eleven commending all and reminding them that Christmas dinner would be at four p.m., dress casual. But he faced this last unfinished business with no more resources and no new ideas.

"Nada! Zip! I should have planned for this," was all he could say in his defense, still getting nowhere.

"At least there weren't so many B's this year," said Egil, trying to look on the bright side. He pointed to the code Santa kept in the big book: the code used to sort out the GOOD and the BAD. Santa was happy that lots of G's this year kept him busy—busier, in fact, than he had ever been. So busy, that now with Christmas Eve not yet over, there was nothing left in his sack. He dug around again, his big hands feeling far into the familiar corners and deep velvety folds. He even searched his pockets.

"NOTHING!"

Three elves woke to the boom of Santa's voice. Outside, bells and hoofbeats ruffled the late night air and from the roof, a soft dust of snow swirled a few feet out and fell on Hector, the house 'guard' cat asleep on the driveway. Some minutes later the jingling died down and the third shift fell back to sleep. Soft, crunching, snow sounds told Santa the reindeer knelt at rest again. And then he noticed it. Over in the corner next to the fireplace broom slumped the sad black bag that held only lumps of coal.

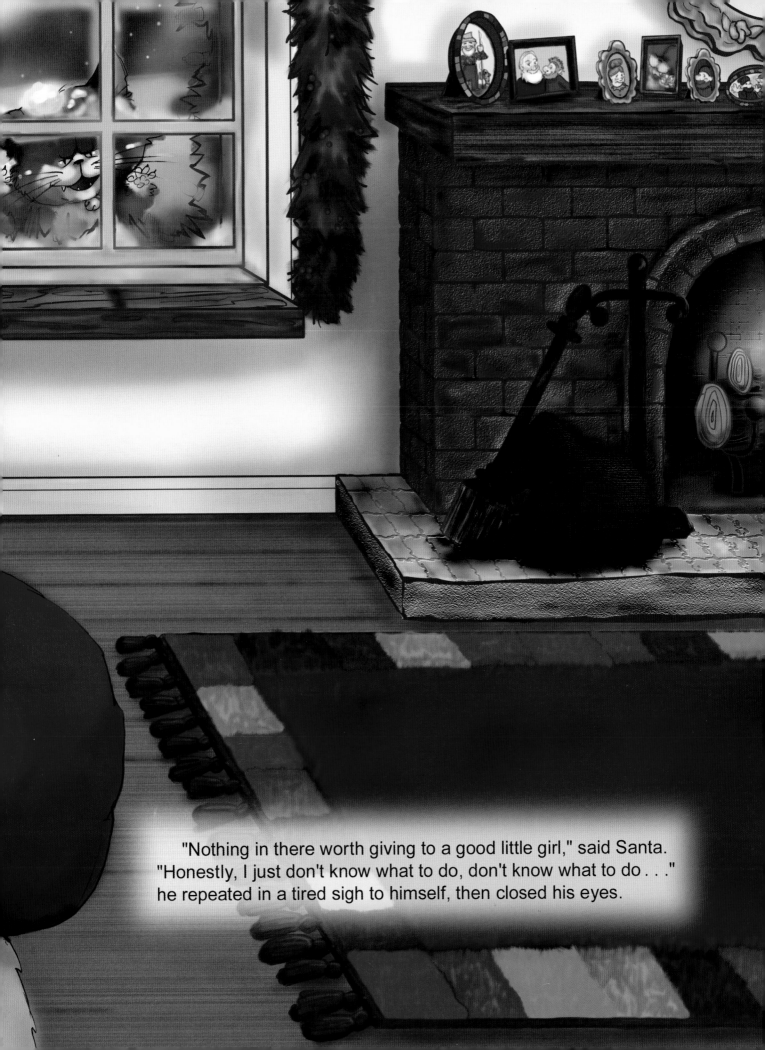

"Nothing in there worth giving to a good little girl," said Santa. "Honestly, I just don't know what to do, don't know what to do . . ." he repeated in a tired sigh to himself, then closed his eyes.

A moment later, as if in answer to an unspoken prayer, an angel appeared and offered one small miracle: *the nature of the situation, the lateness of the hour, the time of the year, etc., etc.*, she explained, demanded action. And Heaven, always generous, had decided to send one of the 'special' gifts.

"Hence, a miracle," said the angel. "But only a small one. Those are my orders."

The angel's name was Gloria. Having explained herself, she was eager to get down to business. Being new to heavenly service, however, and limited in her powers of creation, the angel insisted she must start with something. Surely there was something Santa had. Santa just shook his head. Even his beard was exhausted and refused to sway.

"What about in there?" She pointed to the black bag.

"Oh no," cried Egil. "That's just coal!"

But there was one lump left and that was enough.

"So, tell me Santa, do you know what little Annie wants?" Gloria was beginning to enjoy this. First meeting with the big red man himself and holding her own. *Excellent*, she thought — though her wings were still shaking.

Santa was starting to perk up; his beard visibly stiffened. *Something in the air?* he wondered. The room crackled with a form of energy he'd never felt before.

"Shall I repeat the question?" offered Gloria.

Santa shook his head, this time smiling. He was wide awake now and suddenly everything seemed as it was in his youth, when the world and every moment in it was new and exciting and a wonderful adventure. Then, in the next instant, he remembered the present day and hour and the one task left to complete this night.

Santa had heard Annie's wishes throughout the year, as he heard the wishes of all the girls and boys throughout all the years. *Not a difficult case. Nothing time would not heal,* thought Santa. But he knew some hurts took a long time mending. Like her 'alone times'—crying through the long, winter nights when the wind whips up a frightful noise like high-pitched voices that go on and on and on . . .

A small miracle will be very fine here, thought Santa.

Egil read his mind and grinned. As head elf he had to know everything Santa knew ("well, almost everything," he admitted to another elf one year) and mind-reading was much used on the job.

This is big. Only one gift left to give and a miracle with which to give it! Egil danced wildly at the idea. He would have quite a story to tell generations of elves.

"We've never had a miracle, Santa!" cried Egil.

Santa knew that this was *bigger* than big. He was glad to bring goodwill and cheer and presents, year in and year out, wherever he could. *Absolutely!* He loved it. But the possibilities with a miracle, even a small miracle, were so tremendous . . . had so much potential . . . that he —— Santa paused for a moment, a bit worked-up himself.

"We've never had a miracle, Egil," he finally said.

Egil, having completed his whirl about the room,
now hung straight upside down, his feet planted firmly
on the ceiling. He calmly pulled a little yellow book out
of his pocket and wrote *Christmas Eve, very late—
Santa stressed tonight. Good thing the elves are here.*

The angel broke their reverie.

"Well, I've never had a miracle, either," said Gloria.
"Let's get on with it!"

So Santa told the angel what Annie wanted and the angel gave him a kiss.

"Standard reward," Gloria said, winking at Egil, and in another moment the miracle began.

The small lump of coal the angel held was blacker than jet. But off its rough surface sparkled the firelight. Gloria spoke a few words that only Heaven could hear and the black rock began to tremble. It floated up in an intense unearthly glow, like some soft, dense fog turned electric white. The glow

A whisper of a shape wavered within, but still not a sound. A glow within the glow tried to take form. A blue ribbon of electricity became something familiar—an outline faint at first, until it grew brighter and filled in . . .

. . . and finally emerged as the solid, unmistakable fact of a small black teddy bear. Its short, lustrous fur was marked only by a brown nose, a slim smile and two remarkable hazelnut eyes.

"Oh my!" cried Egil. The hazelnut eyes were that remarkable.

"That's one nice teddy." Santa could see that plainly. *No other teddy bear quite like this one*, he thought.

"What does he do? What does he do?" cried Egil.

All eyes were now on Gloria. This was getting good!

But in the next instant they were in a little room, half-a-world away, where they found Annie asleep in her bed. The black bear was still aloft and staring at a cloud-covered moon painted on Annie's ceiling. Santa and Egil just looked at each other and then at the angel.

"Well, you said there wasn't much time," justified Gloria. Santa was impressed. She was right, of course; it was almost morning now. But he wanted to know more — about her, how she traveled, how she knew Annie's name. After hearing the answers, Egil made another note in his little yellow book, *Read Einstein again.*

Then the angel spoke once more:

"Little bear, stay with Annie now. In the morning, when first light comes, whisper your name. Share her secrets and her worries. Share her sadness and her joy. Above all, share your love. Tonight you have been given something wonderful to give of yourself: a love that will never die. It is a love that forever heals and comforts. It is a love that strengthens the heart. It is a love that will enlighten and inspire. Stay with her always, little Percy bear."

And when the angel kissed him goodbye, Percy floated into Annie's bed under the soft covers and snuggled up close, his furry ears just touching her cheek. He did not go to sleep, nor could he. He felt for the first time this little girl's arms around him and she felt warm. He could also feel his heart touching her heart and when Annie gave a little squeeze, Percy had to lay very still. *Not long now*, he said to himself. *Not long now*. And just at dawn, when he thought she would wake, Percy gently whispered his name.

Precisely as instructed.